A CROW

CALLED

CAN★UCK

by Arran & Haru Yarmie

in association with

The Hancock Wildlife Foundation
www.hancockwildlife.org

ISBN-13: 978-0-88839-106-3 [trade edition softcover]

Cataloging in Publication Data

Yarmie, Arran, author, illustrator
A crow called Canuck / by Arran Yarmie.

"In association with The Hancock Wildlife Foundation".
Activities follow main text.
Illustrated by Arran Yarmie and Haru Muraki Yarmie.
ISBN 978-0-88839-106-3 (softcover)

I. Yarmie, Haru Muraki, illustrator II. Hancock Wildlife
Foundation III. Title. IV. Title: Canuck the crow.

PS8647.A76C76 2019   jC813'.6   C2018-906346-7

Printed in the USA

All illustrations © Arran Yarmie & Haru Muraki Yarmie unless noted otherwise

Cover Illustrations © Arran & Haru Yarmie
Back cover: "Canuck" on car mirror by Linda A. Martin

Partial proceeds from the sale of this title will go towards the Hancock Wildlife Foundation to help further our education and research programs.

Please visit www.hancockwildlife.org for more information

Hancock House gratefully acknowledges the Semiahmoo, Kwantlen and Katzie First Nations, whose unceded traditional territories our offices reside upon.

Published simultaneously in Canada and the United States by
HANCOCK HOUSE PUBLISHERS LTD.
19313 Zero Avenue, Surrey, B.C. Canada V3Z 9R9
(604) 538-1114   Fax (604) 538-2262

HANCOCK HOUSE PUBLISHERS
#104-4550 Birch Bay-Lynden Rd, Blaine, WA U.S.A. 98230-9436
(800) 938-1114   Fax (800) 983-2262

www.hancockhouse.com   sales@hancockhouse.com

THE STORY OF CANUCK

He was once an orphan but became a celebrity and is the Unofficial Ambassador of Vancouver. It's Canuck the Crow! The story of how a fledgling crow rose to become a media and internet sensation is a tale that deserves to be told.

It all started in a quiet neighbourhood in East Vancouver. Who could have known that when a family found and raised an abandoned crow, it would set off a chain of events that would make a common crow into an extraordinary public figure. Soon after the family released the crow with an orange band on his ankle back into his natural surroundings, he started exhibiting some human behaviours that attracted a lot of media attention.

Some of his antics have been caught on film and featured on news broadcasts across the province and the nation. Stealing a knife from a crime scene, taking a SkyTrain to a shopping mall and dining on fries in a fast food restaurant are a few of Canuck's mischiefs that made him a household name. When not making headlines, Canuck often spends time with his crow and human friends. He even has his own Facebook page with thousands of followers. In a CBC online poll, Canuck received the most votes beating out local personalities the likes of former mayor Gregor Robertson, Michael J. Fox and Seth Rogan to be the Unofficial Ambassador of Vancouver!

It may seem humorous that a crow could be the representative of a city, but he is the perfect ambassador for Vancouver. He's touched many people's lives in countless ways. In a multicultural city such as Vancouver where people from all walks of life not only coexist, but thrive together, it's fitting that Ambassador Canuck has shown us humans how we can do the same with urban wildlife. This book also tells the story of some of the challenges facing wildlife near large cities and the struggles they face.

Publishers Note: It is a breach of the BC Wildlife Act to take wildlife home.
Please always contact your local wildlife rehab facility if you find an orphaned or injured animal.

In a quiet neighborhood, outside the bustling city of Vancouver, a baby crow was born.

The crow was loved and cared for
by his parents.

One day, a windstorm knocked the crow out of his nest. His parents could not help him get back to his home.

6

The baby crow was now all alone in the big city world.

A human family found the abandoned crow and took him to their house.

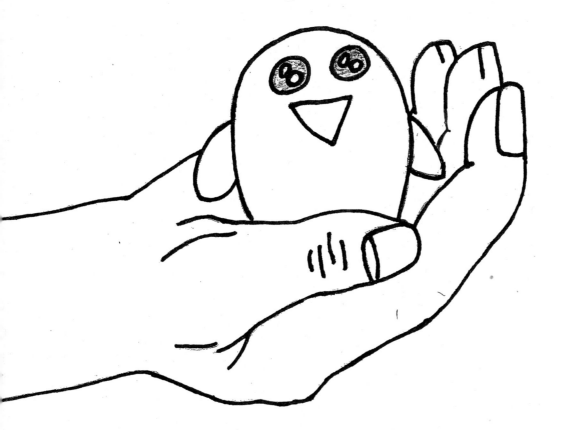

The family took care of the crow until he was strong enough to live on his own.

Before they released him , they put an orange band on his ankle so they knew it was him, and gave him the name Canuck.

Now, all grown up, Canuck goes on many adventures around the city.

Canuck loves to explore and be around people, often spending time in his neighbourhood.

School playgrounds, baseball fields and soccer pitches are places Canuck likes to be near people.

One day, Canuck followed some people into
a restaurant and helped himself
to human food.

He had no manners because he was raised
by humans and not his parents.

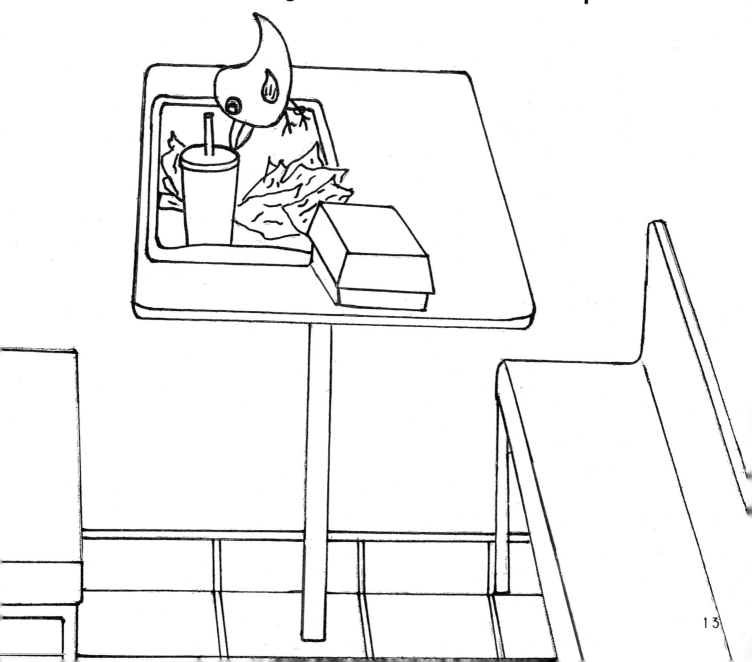

Canuck has even ridden the SkyTrain
to the shopping mall!

Many people take photos and videos of Canuck on their phones.

Canuck has become famous and has been on the news and TV many times.

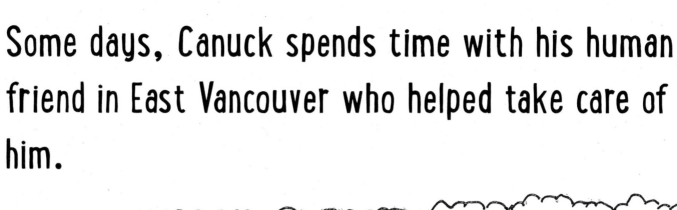

Some days, Canuck spends time with his human friend in East Vancouver who helped take care of him.

He often sits on his arm and gets a head rub while hearing of some of the dangers of living in a big city.

Canuck is very curious about people because he wasn't raised by his parents.

Sometimes this gets him into trouble.

Once while Canuck was visiting a soccer game, a man tried to chase him away with a pole. Canuck was injured in the head and hurt very badly.

Canuck's human friend rushed him to the animal hospital.

He was treated for his injuries and released a few days later. Canuck was lucky to survive and learned a valuable lesson.

Soon after Canuck recovered, he was back to his old tricks.

WARNING
CANUCK
ON DUTY

He would often swoop down
near people's heads when
they came near his old nest
to guard his territory.

A mail carrier had to stop delivering mail to a few houses in Canuck's territory for a month because he kept dive bombing and pecking him!

Because Canuck was not raised by his wild parents, he was no longer afraid of humans like most wild birds are and behaved badly.

The mail carrier didn't give up trying to deliver the mail to the houses, though.

One day Canuck landed on the mail carrier's arm and he realized he could be Canuck's friend instead of his enemy.

24

Canuck and the mail carrier are now friends. The mail carrier can once again deliver mail to all the houses near Canuck's nest.

Now that trust has been built between the two friends, Canuck will often land on the mail carrier's arm and the two will spend time together.

Canuck has even sat in the passenger seat of the mail carrier's delivery van and helped with the mail route!

Canuck has a mate called Cassiar.

They had two chicks, who unfortunately did not survive the dangers of the big city. Canuck and Cassiar hope they can try again next spring.

At night, Canuck joins his friends in Burnaby where they all sleep at night in a large group called a "rookery".

But he hears whispers that all is not well with wildlife near the city.

30

Canuck decides to visit his friend Bald Eagle in Delta, to find out what is going on. They tell him about how they are losing trees to nest in because so many are cut down and turned into houses for people.

You can watch our live streaming cameras of Bald Eagles and other wildlife at hancockwildlife.org

He then flies to North Vancouver and talks to Black Bear.

He has to look for food in garbage cans because his forest home is disappearing and very few salmon are coming back to the Capilano river where he hunts for fish.

33

Canuck then goes to visit Barn Owl south of the Fraser River.

Barn Owl tells him about how his fields where he hunts mice are being turned into cities and the mice here are often poisoned which makes his babies sick.

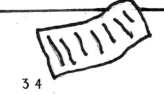

34

Canuck then flies home to the city. He finds out that Raccoon and some other wildlife can adjust to life in the busy city.

City life is often dangerous for wildlife and they must be careful.

Canuck has learned some valuable lessons over the last few years about life for wildlife in an urban city. Like many of his friends, some have adapted well and others still face challenges.

It is up to us as humans, to make sure we preserve and protect wildlife and their environments for future generations.

Who knows what adventures Canuck will get up to next. You might even be the next one to have an encounter with him.

If you see a crow with an orange band on his leg, give him some space and say hello!

Canuck Questions

1. Why did a human family look after Canuck?

_____

2. How did the human family make sure they could recognize Canuck after they released him?

_____

3. Where did Canuck sneak into to get some food?

_____

4. Why did Canuck get hurt?

_____

5. Where was Canuck taken after he got hurt?

_____

6. How did Canuck become friends with a mail carrier?

_____

7. What problem do bald eagles have in Delta?

_____

8. What types of wild animals can you see in the city?

_____

9. If you see a wild animal, why should you not go close to it?

_____

10.   What can people do to help protect wildlife?

_____

Canuck the Crow Word Search
Find the key words from the story in the puzzle

```
N G I Q H Q A O K B H S L F I U K S M K
T P A R L X I E S J B X R S R C Z B S Y
G Y W Y J Q G R Y E W S J L R M W X U G
G J C S C A N U C K H O G J Z R J Z H I
U F R I E N D T B J O T R A Q E K L G C
W D Y A R O O N P Y S G O C N B N R V H
B D R H O S J E B O P E G B I Y U O D X
N I H E L V G V C Y I B N G L L D E L S
Y R Y O P G A D F O T R U H P F B R M A
S K Q N X V C A L F A Q G D W P V E Z B
G K N E E B L U M S L K E A E A V Y M A
I X Y S Y M N K M L T B R N X D W C A H
T Z W T V O C Z V S D U L H T F E H A T
K N R A R K C K N N I S G Z A T Z T V X
A E T S N A H J O G K G A F D Q N N H M
Q S Y K I G I J X V O F A Y I Z X E N N
I T J L Y N I N A B D I Y U Y E X K N M
O O Q M Y H S U C K O F M C O E S D Z V
B A R H K C W K G O H I S X T L R T G Z
U H X A F K N Z P U L E O N K X T F Y L
```

CANUCK	CROW	HURT
ALONE	ADVENTURE	EXPLORE
FRIEND	HOSPITAL	NEST
SKYTRAIN	FIESTY	FLY

HOW MANY WORDS CAN YOU MAKE OUT OF

CANUCK THE CROW?

1. Know

2. _____

3. _____

4. _____

5. _____

6. _____

7. _____

8. _____

9. _____

10. _____

11. _____

12. _____

13. _____

14. _____

15. _____

Crow Vocabulary

1. A group of crows is called a **flock** or **murder**

2. A baby crow is called a **chick**.

3. A large bird that looks like a crow is called a **raven**.

4. A place with many nests grouped together is called a **rookery**.

5. A person who studies birds is called an **ornithologist**.

Can you say ornithologist five times fast?

Crow Quiz

Cover the vocabulary page and take the quiz.

1. What is a baby crow called? _____

2. What is a large bird that looks like a crow called?_____

3. What is a place with many nests grouped together called?

_____

4. What is a group of crows called?

_____

5. What is a person who studies birds called? _____

Canuck the Crow Crossword

Complete the crossword below

Across

2. Where Canuck went when he was injured.
4. A baby crow hatches from one.
6. Canuck snuck in and ate some food.
8. The colour of crows.
9. Canuck sat it the passenger seat of one.

Down

1. Canuck was injured by it.
3. Canuck took a ride on one.
5. The place where Canuck sits on his human friend
7. A place where crows are born.
8. Canuck has one on his leg.

Wildlife Matching

Put the letter beside the description by the name of the wild animal that can be found in the Lower Mainland.

1._____ crow

2._____ pigeon

3._____ eagle

4._____ heron

5._____ squirrel

6._____ rat

7._____ cougar

8._____ coyote

9._____ seal

10._____ raccoon

11._____ seagull

12._____ duck

13._____ bear

A. It looks like a dog.

B. A large bird with a white head.

C. It swims in the ocean.

D. Canuck is one.

E. A tall slim bird with a long beak.

F. A white bird that likes to be by the sea.

G. A large animal with brown or black fur.

H. It has a long fluffy tail.

I. It looks like a large mouse.

J. A large type of cat.

K. A brown bird that has webbed feet.

L. It has black marks around its eyes.

M. A small grey bird with a long neck.

1. D 2. M 3. B 4. E 5. H 6. I 7. J 8. A 9. C 10. L 11. F 12. K 13. G

Answers

Think of words that start with letters in the name Canuck.

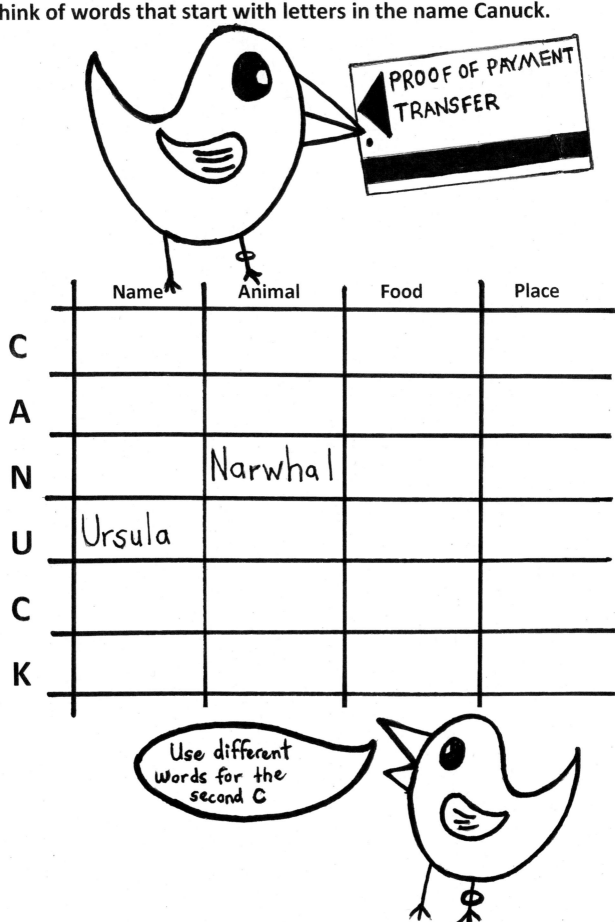

	Name	Animal	Food	Place
C				
A				
N		Narwhal		
U	Ursula			
C				
K				

Use different words for the second C

PROOF OF PAYMENT TRANSFER

Use the code to find the message

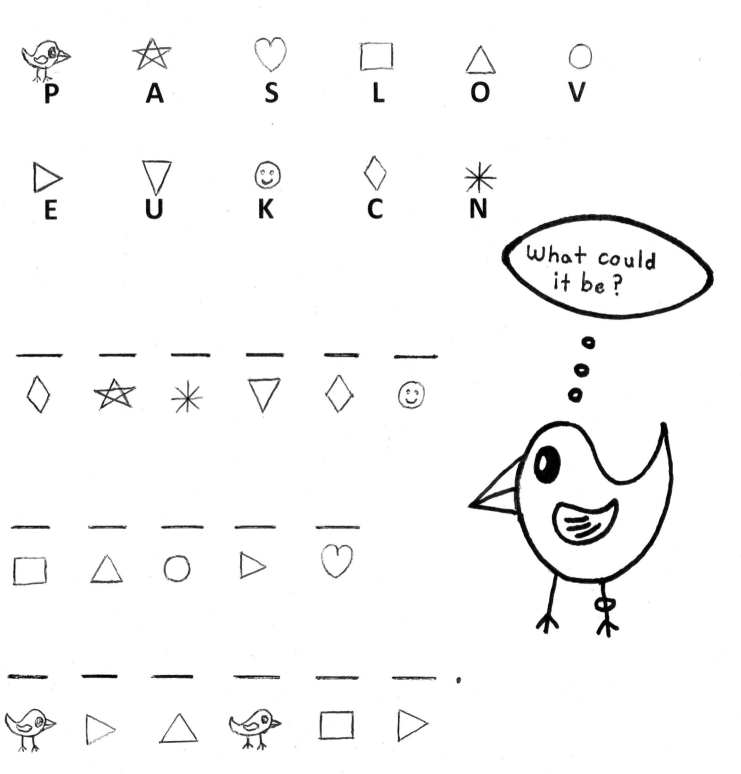

P A S L O V

E U K C N

What could it be?

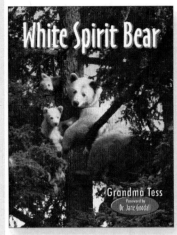
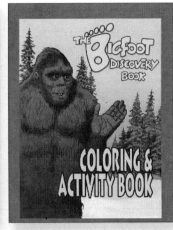

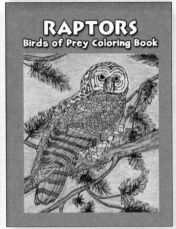

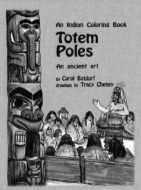
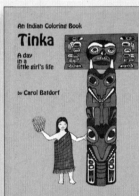